NELL
AND THE
CAVE BEAR

First published in Great Britain in 2021 by
PICCADILLY PRESS
80-81 Wimpole Street, London W1G 9RE
Owned by Bonnier Books
Sveavägen 56, Stockholm, Sweden

A CIP catalogue record for this book is available from the British Library.

ISBN: 9781848129689

1

This book is typeset in Bembo MT Schoolbook

Printed and bound in China.

MIX
Paper from
responsible sources
FSC® C020056

Piccadilly Press is an imprint of Bonnier Books UK

Hot Key Books is part of the Bonnier Publishing Group
www.**bonnierbooks**.co.uk

Edited by Felicity Alexander, Jenny Jacoby and Maurice Lyon
Designed by Dominica Clements
Copy-edited by Jennie Roman
Proofread by Jane Hammett
Production by Emma Kidd

NELL
AND THE
CAVE BEAR

MARTIN BROWN

Piccadilly
PRESS

To my dad

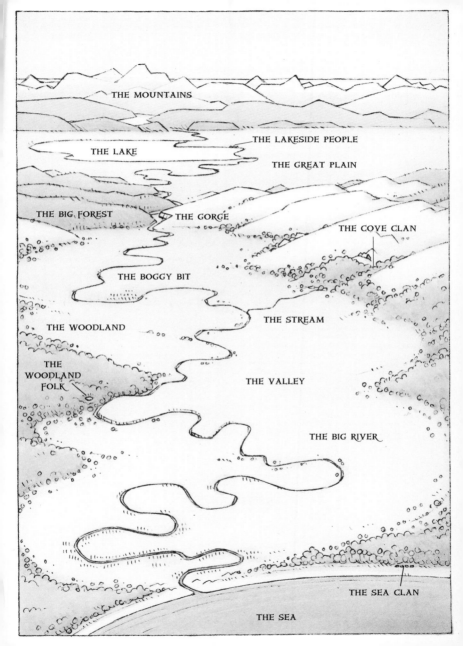

It was a long, long time ago, when the land beyond the mountains was an everlasting sea of ice.

But below the mountains the hard winter was over. Spring had finally come to the valley and the melting snow released a thunderous torrent of water into the river. Along its banks the water dug at the earth and pulled at the reeds, swallowing soil and rocks and plants alike, turning the wave-peaked surge a dull muddy brown.

'*Meow.*'

At the edge of the big forest the trunk of an old tree was losing its grip on the disappearing riverside. Slowly it began to lean over, inch by inch, first one stumpy root giving up on the ground, then another. It bent further and further towards the rushing water, until it seemed to hover, horizontal, between falling and fallen, between land and stream. Then, at last, almost without a sound, it sank into the river where the mighty current tore it from the bank as if it were little more than a twig.

Rolling and twisting, the ancient tree was swept away in the flood, just a few roots and some short branches showing . . . and its single occupant wondering what the heck was going on.

1

Everyone at the cave was busy. Bright
morning sunshine lit the valley and poured
into the broad open space, illuminating the
bustling activity inside. Woolly rugs were
beaten and the dusty earthen floor swept.
Rubbish that had piled up over the long
winter months was carried out

and down to the heap. Fresh reeds and ferns for bedding were brought in. Bone needles were being used to repair clothes while the flint makers chipped away at new axes and spearheads.

There was a lot to do. Not only did the cave need a good spring clean, the people living there, amongst the scattered trees and rocky outcrops, needed to prepare for their annual trip to the hunting grounds up on the great plain.

But there was an extra buzz in the air. In just a little while their seaside cousins were coming for a visit.

It was always a special occasion when the Cave Clan and the Sea Clan got together. It didn't happen very often. The weather had to be just right to allow for the long trek up or down the valley. If the snows melted too late, no one would be able to get through. If spring came early, the Cave Clan would have already left to follow the hunt. If there were storms, the Sea Clan had to stay to protect their boats and huts. And they'd also stay if the ocean was calm and the fishing was good.

So everyone was busy. Mums were trying to tidy and pack

and make things look welcoming while
also attempting to look after the toddlers
and babies, who all seemed to start running
around or need changing at precisely the
same time. The older folk were talking
a lot, planning the feast and the sleeping
arrangements and remembering when the
seaside relatives were here last. The young
men sat in the sunshine checking their
new flint weapons and chatting about the
upcoming hunting season. In the centre
of all the activity stood Mayv, older, wiser
and slightly fatter than the others, sternly
directing operations and making sure
everybody had a job to do.

Perhaps the busiest of all was Nell and
her pet cave-bear cub, who had never

found a better name than Cave Bear. It seemed every grown-up in the cave wanted Nell to do something just for them. Gordn wanted her to get more firewood. Feeona wanted help with the little ones. Soo needed the baskets of bones emptied. Kehn told her to sweep up all the chips left over from chipping flints. There were fur rugs to shake, food to put away and water to fetch.

When you don't have a mum and dad, everyone

else steps in to be your mum and dad instead. That's great when it's stories and cuddles, but not so good when it's work and chores. The other children all seemed to be much older or younger than her. The young ones were either too young to help or old enough to be a nuisance. The bigger kids seemed to have sneaked off and were nowhere to be seen. That left Nell and Cave Bear to be everyone's helper. Not that a bear cub could help that much. He tried, tugging at rugs or dragging pieces of wood, but it was Nell who did most of the sweeping, cleaning, fetching and carrying.

For the third time that morning Nell trudged down the sloping apron of rock that was the cave's terrace and front porch, this time grabbing a satchel of food as she went. At the bottom, with Cave Bear at her heels, she turned left along the path through the bushes to the little area of overhanging rock where the spring came out from beneath the boulders and collected in a crystal-clear pool. From there she could hear everything going on above her in the cave, but couldn't be seen.

'That's it,' she said to Cave Bear. 'I'm having a break. All I've done this morning is work. The other kids are either hiding or hopeless. I'm the only one doing anything.

Just because I don't have a mum or dad doesn't mean they can all boss me around like they're all my parents. It's not fair.'

Cave Bear looked at Nell with a very understanding expression.

'It's not my fault my mum got sick and my dad got frozen.' She slumped on to a mossy rock and took out some nuts and dried meat for them both to nibble on. Even though she was a bit put out, Nell was rarely sad. She couldn't remember her father and mother at all. The tribe had been all the family she'd ever known and she wouldn't stay cross with them for long. But thank goodness for Cave Bear – he was the best friend a girl could have.

'OK, little chum, rant over. Back to work.'

She slung the food satchel over her shoulder, untied the drawstrings of the water bags and began to dip them in the water.

Above her on the sloping rock, in the vast entrance to the cave, Mayv was talking to the older clan members about the upcoming visit. 'There'll be more than enough room in the cave if we all budge up a bit, but we'll have to dig out those old furs for extra bedding. And we still have to decide what we're having for the feast. Something better than dried elk would be nice.'

'And presents,' added Porl. 'It's a tradition. Last time, when we went to them, they gave us loads of stuff.'

'Mostly fish,' said Moyrra.

'Yeah, mostly fish,' mumbled the others.

Mayv held up her hand to stop the grumbling. 'I've been thinking about that. I've got an idea. It's not perfect, but it's probably better than fish.'

At that moment Leeum, one of the hunters, ran, panting, up to the cave.

'There are mammoths in the valley,' he gasped.

Everyone stopped what they were doing and turned to look.

'Mammoths? Mammoths? In our valley? Are you sure?' asked Mayv.

'I'm sure,' wheezed Leeum, leaning on his spear.

Mayv looked doubtful. 'Big brown fluffy things?'

'Yes, mammoths, mammoths! All huge and tusky and huge.'

'Well, well,' said Mayv with a thoughtful look on her lined, round face. 'There haven't been mammoths in the valley for years. This is brilliant!'

'Brilliant?'

'Brilliant, absolutely. Think of the furs

and ivory and all the meat. It's ideal with
the Sea Clan coming. A bit of hunting right
here in the valley, then lots of new woolly
skins to sleep on, tons of food, and we can
send them home with all sorts of generous
mammoth goodies. Definitely better than
fish.'

'Much better than fish,' agreed the others.

'I suppose,' said a reluctant-looking
Leeum. 'But we haven't gone after
mammoths for ages. Some of the younger
hunters never have. It's a big deal,
mammoths. They're tricky, and . . . huge.
What if we don't get anything?'

'You'll be fine. You're hunters, aren't
you?' said Mayv confidently. 'Besides, we've
always got that old elk we were saving

and we can give them that present I was thinking of before you showed up and told us about all those lovely big mammoths.'

'What was that?' asked Leeum.

'Well, apart from fish, I know our seaside cousins love pets. So I was planning to give them that stumpy little cave bear cub that follows Nell around all the time.'

Down by the spring, Nell froze.

2

Nell and Cave Bear had been together
ever since she had found him hiding in
the deepest part of the cave when she'd
returned with the clan after last year's
hunting season. Curled up in a corner, he
was just a tiny, hungry, frightened bundle
of fur.

Nell had immediately known there
was something different about him. Bear
cubs were usually born during the winter
and emerged with their mothers after

hibernation in the spring. This cub must have been born just a few weeks before in the summer. And there was no sign of his mum. Perhaps that's why he was so small, even for a cub.

All through the long winter Nell nursed the baby bear back to health. Now he was a not-so-frightened, not-so-hungry and not-so-tiny bundle of fur – and Nell's best friend. It looked as though Cave Bear was always going to be small, but that was no bad thing.

Some of the others in the clan were not sure about having a cave bear in the cave. Generally, as bears got older they got bigger. Much bigger. And no one was convinced that a young girl with a ten-foot-tall pet bear was a good idea. Several senior members of the tribe, and Mayv in particular, thought that it could only end in disaster. But the mums and dads who had been closest to Nell's parents, and who had cared for her when she was little, were more understanding. The lonely orphan had a friend and she was happy. And that was lovely to see.

Halfway down the cave, sitting round a fire, the hunters were having a meeting. Daev, a wiry, tired-looking man and one of the more experienced huntsmen, started the ball rolling. 'OK, how do you think we should do this?'

Caal, another of the older hunters, stood up. 'We could do it the way we did it before. Chase one into the boggy bit by the big river. It gets stuck and it's easier to spear. Simple.'

The other men nodded with approval. They liked the idea of it being simple, especially Dann, who had never hunted anything bigger than a deer.

'Yeah, it's simple,' replied Daev. 'But then you've got an enormous great lump of dead mammoth in a swamp. Remember the last time? It took ages to get the meat off the thing and even then we had to leave half of it behind because it was under water.'

The other men nodded, remembering. 'We nearly lost Gordn in that goo,' said Leeum.

Aydn, another younger man, spoke up. 'Why not chase them the other way? Up the valley. We could trap them in the gorge or even chase one off the cliffs.'

Dann looked hopeful. 'That might work!'

Leeum looked less hopeful. 'But it's miles away. We'd be gone even longer. And carrying the meat and everything all the way back? We'd still have to leave most of it behind.'

More nodding.

'Right,' said Daev. 'This is what I think. I say, as the mammoths come down the valley, we spear one as soon as we can, with as many spears as we can, to weaken it. Then chase it until it collapses. Hopefully it won't be too far away. With any luck we'll be done by tonight, the cave will be full of mammoth stuff and we'll be back here, round this very fire.'

'Sounds good to me,' said Caal.

'Me too,' agreed Dann eagerly.

'Great,' said the others, standing up.

Daev scratched his nose. 'There is one downside to the plan.'

The hunters stopped.

'Instead of weakening the mammoth we might just injure it enough to make it really cross. And it could, I suppose, turn round and kill us all.'

'Oh,' said Dann.

Under the overhanging rock Nell had also been wondering what to do. But nothing came into her head. It was too full. Anger at Mayv, worry about the chances of the hunters and despair at the thought of losing

Cave Bear all whizzed around her brain in equal measure.

She cuddled her beloved friend close to her and stared at the dancing reflections on the little pool, rippling as the spring trickled in at one end and out into the tiniest of streams at the other. Trickling in and trickling out, running away from the pool, into the woods, away from the cave.

'It's running away, Cave Bear,' she sighed. Then she added, 'Running away! Cave Bear, that's it! If the water can run away, so can we. I don't know where it's going, but it's not staying here. And if Mayv and the others are going to give you away, then we shouldn't stay either. We'll follow the water. Wherever it goes, we'll go. Into the woods, away from the cave!'

She adjusted the strap of the food bag and stepped across to where the pool became the little stream. 'We have everything we need. Are you ready, Cave Bear?'

Cave Bear looked up at her with a determined expression, which Nell took to mean 'Absolutely!'

They looked to see where the bubbling thread of water had gone and stepped into the ferns and shadows.

3

Up on the terrace the cave families had gathered to see the hunters set off, each man laden with spears and bags.

'Bring us back some lovely mammoth goodies,' called Mayv to the departing men.

'Happy hunting!' cried everyone else.

'I'll be happy if we all don't get killed,' muttered Dann.

Mayv turned to go back inside. 'You'll be fine.'

The cave opened like a great bay of air in the projecting slabs of rock. Above it the ground rose with the hill to a ragged ridge and in front it fell away in a covering of trees to the broad green valley beyond. Further up the valley the line of hills closed in on the river, forcing it to tumble through a deep canyon. Past that lay the big forest and, further still, the great plain and its icy lake, all overlooked by the high white mountains. Down the valley,

through meadow, wetland and woodland, the river slowed and widened and snaked its way to the sea. Not many people lived in this wild landscape. Those that did hunted the animals they shared it with. The Cave Clan

stalked the herds of the open plains, the Sea Clan fished the sea. The Lakeside people lived off geese and eels. But

the Woodland lot hunted anything: bird, boar, badger or bear – especially bear.

As Nell and Cave Bear picked their way downhill, the Cave Clan hunters were walking across the same hillside, but up towards the higher heath-covered slopes of the valley where Leeum had seen the mammoths.

'Are we nearly there yet?' said Dann.

'Shhhh!' said Daev over his shoulder from the front of the line of men.

'It's just that I'd like to know how worried I should be getting.'

'Shhhh!' said Leeum. 'It's not far now – just below those rocks up ahead. We'll have to be quiet from now on.'

The Cave Clan men crept down the slope to a cluster of boulders and lay side by side on a flat rock that overlooked the valley floor like a balcony. Below them were scattered twenty or more mammoths, pulling at the fresh spring grasses with the tips of their trunks or calmly twisting branches off low bushes, almost absent-mindedly swinging the clumps and leaves up into their mouths.

They were immense. Even the small ones were big. The only way the tallest man in the clan could look the biggest mammoth in the eye was if he was standing on the shoulders of the second-tallest man in the clan.

Their massive sides rose like shaggy walls resting on furry tree trunks. Mighty tusks swept down and out and up in pale graceful arcs. Some were so large that the tallest man and the second-tallest man would need a third man if they were ever planning to carry one back to the cave.

The mammoths were quietly moving over the valley floor as they grazed, occasionally greeting each other with a raised trunk or a low rumble that the watching hunters could feel rather than hear.

The men raised their heads slowly to peer at the great beasts below.

'Let's not pick a big one that will kill us.' Dann was staring intently at one that seemed even bigger than the others. 'And not a small one because its mum might kill us.'

'How about a medium one, then? That brown one there,' said Aydn, pointing to the middle of the herd.

'They're all brown,' said Leeum.

Daev seemed to be shaking his
head to himself. 'OK, OK. Let's not spend
the entire day picking mammoths. We'll
go for the medium one there near the bush,
the one with the small tusks and big ears.
Everyone see it?'

There was some nodding and general
mumbles of understanding.

'Great. Kehn, take Aydn, Roj, Dann and
Murri down into that thicket and get ready.
Us three will circle round behind the herd.

We'll stand up, shout and wave and spook them into moving. We'll chase them right past you. When the mammoth we want goes by, throw your spears, and then we'll throw ours. We'll follow it down the valley, throw some more spears, and hopefully it won't take long for it to fall over. Got that?'

More mumbles of understanding.

'OK. Let's go.'

The eight men shuffled backwards off the rock so as not to be seen from below. Then they crouched up and started to move into position.

'Remember,' whispered Daev. 'Small tusks, big ears.'

4

Nell had been in the woods below the cave dozens of times before, but it had always been with adults, collecting food or firewood. She'd grown up learning what to gather. What was good to eat and what was useful. The world around them provided everything you could need. All you had to do was know where to look. But now she and Cave Bear were on their own. Not that she minded. She didn't really want to be around any grown-ups just now.

'Hmmf, Cave Bear. What gives them the right to give you away? You're not theirs to hand over to any scraggy relative that comes along. It's not fair. It's not right.'

Cave Bear looked cross too.

'Running away is the best thing to do. Right now they'll be wondering where we are and worrying and sending someone out after us. But I won't go back. No way. Not till they promise you can stay.'

Nell and Cave Bear continued to pick their way through the bracken and bushes, following the path of the tiny stream as it wriggled down the mossy slope. It was so small that sometimes it would disappear completely under rocks and logs or get lost in clumps of grass, but Cave Bear would always find it again. Down and down they went, away from the cave, away from home. Soon they noticed a second tiny ribbon of water flowing into the trickle they had been following.

'Two streams, Cave Bear. I wonder where that one's running away from?' She'd forgotten she was supposed to be angry; now she was just curious. 'They're running away together.'

The two trickles joined to make a slightly bigger, faster trickle. To keep up with the water they had to keep going, tracking the trickle like hunters. Then a third stream met theirs, and before long a fourth. Each one added to the one before so that now the little trickle jumped and splashed and

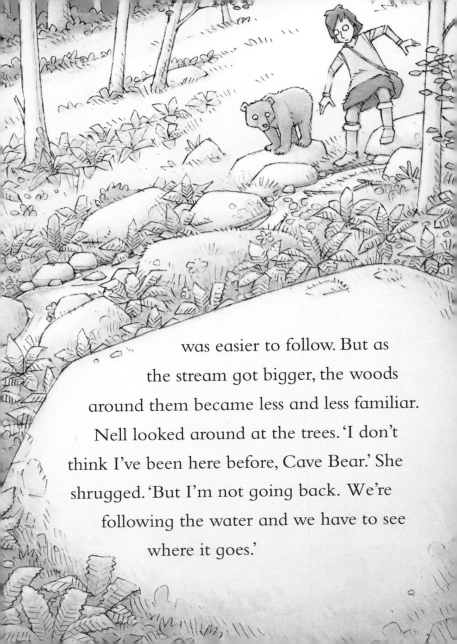

was easier to follow. But as
the stream got bigger, the woods
around them became less and less familiar.
Nell looked around at the trees. 'I don't
think I've been here before, Cave Bear.' She
shrugged. 'But I'm not going back. We're
following the water and we have to see
where it goes.'

Nell and Cave Bear had started out
at the cave as runaways; now they were
explorers. They didn't have to hunt for the
trickle any more, as it had grown into a
babbling brook. The water was white and
wild when rushing over stones and boulders,
then dark and silent when it slowed down
into pools, its black surface mirroring the
canopy of bright spring leaves above.

Cave Bear paused to have a drink at
the edge of another pool. Nell looked left
and right at the stream flowing in and out
again. 'It's like the pond at the cave, Cave
Bear, only bigger. The water comes in,
stays for a while, then goes off again. But
where? And is this our water? It's all mixed
up now. One bit of water looks pretty much

like another.' She sat next to her friend
in the dots and dashes of dappled light. A
leaf drifted by, turning gently in the slow
current. Cave Bear stood back from the
stream's edge, watching, then, with a glance
back at Nell, began walking along the
bank, keeping pace with it.

Nell jumped up.
'You clever bear! That's
much easier. Instead of
trying to watch the
water, we can watch
something carried by the
water.' She ran to catch
up and together they
followed the leaf as it
floated down the pool.

Soon rocks broke the calm surface and the leaf bobbled and spun as the water rippled and waved and rushed into a stream again.

'It's too hard to see,' said Nell, struggling to keep sight of the leaf in the bouncing light.

Then, with a whoosh, it disappeared altogether under a great stone slab that had fallen across the brook like a bridge.

'We'll get something else to follow, something easier to keep track of.'

After a quick search, Cave Bear had an old fir cone and Nell a couple of sticks.

'Let's use these.' She gave a stick to Cave Bear.

They stepped up on to the slab bridge and held their sticks out over the water.

'This is where the leaf disappeared so this is where we'll start. Are you ready? Go!'

Both sticks hit the water and vanished under the rock. Nell and Cave Bear hurried across to the other side to see the sticks emerge. 'This could be a game, Cave Bear. We can see whose stick comes out first.'

But, as they watched, both sticks appeared exactly at the same time.

'Oh well, perhaps not.'

In a moment the sticks were swept downstream.

'Quick! After them,' cried Nell, leaping off the slab and along the bank. 'We have to keep up.'

The two runaway explorers dashed through ferns and over rocks beside the

brook. It was bigger now and noisier too —
a constant rushing burble.

The way was often blocked on one side
so they had to cross to the other. Sometimes
there were stepping stones, sometimes they
had to jump, but down the hill they raced.
Once or twice the sticks caught on weeds
or the stream slowed into a pool so the
runners could catch their ragged breaths.
But then the pool broke into a brook again
or the sticks unsnagged and Nell and Cave
Bear were off once more, following their
bobbing marks on the water.

The wood was thinning as they ran.
More sky was above them, more scrubby
bush beside. The weak little trickle was
now a powerful stream. The water ran deep

and fast. Strong currents formed ridges and furrows. Nell and Cave Bear could only just glimpse their sticks now and again in the swirling mix. Then a jumble of boulders ahead shaped the stream into a low waterfall. It boomed and hissed. The sticks shot into the misty white foam and disappeared.

Nell and Cave Bear gazed out from the rocks beside the falls. 'Oh well. At least our little sticks got us to here.'

And here was pretty spectacular. In front of them was the wide expanse of the valley floodplain – bright green with new spring grass and dotted all over with carpets of wild flowers. In the distance they could see deer and wild cattle grazing in the sunshine. Beyond them was the great river itself.

'Is that where the water is going, do you think, Cave Bear? All the way down the hill, little streams were joining other little streams to make bigger streams. And now, look, this bigger stream is heading over to join the biggest stream of all. Is that it? Does water like to be with other water? So it's always on the move – searching for more.'

Cave Bear looked thoughtful.

'I'm glad you agree,' said Nell. 'Let's go and look.'

They clambered

down the boulders and down the slope, past the last few bushy shrubs and out on to the open grassland.

The grass was long and full of buzzing insects. The sun was high and strong and suddenly it occurred to Nell that they hadn't stopped walking since leaving the cave. They stood at the edge of their stream and stared at the cool flowing water.

'Perhaps we could take a break. What do you think, Cave Bear?'

The grassy bank looked soft, the sky was blue and the noise of the waterfall now no more than a rumble you could feel through your feet. A soothing, rhythmic rumble. The sort of rumble you could fall asleep to. Except that it was getting louder.

'That's odd,' said Nell.

She looked hard at the water, trying to concentrate on the growing sound. She looked down at Cave Bear then down towards the river then back up at the waterfall. The sound didn't seem to be coming from the stream at all. And now it was less of a rumble and more a growing thud, thud, thud. A rushing, booming thud, thud, thud. Like something big was coming through long grass.

Nell spun round – the blue sky was black with a gigantic charging mammoth. It trumpeted a fearsome roar and swung its immense tusks to one side, ready to swipe Nell and Cave Bear out of the way – and out of the world forever.

In sheer terror Nell and Cave Bear stepped backwards and fell into the fast-flowing stream. In an instant they were swept away as the enormous beast crashed through the bank where they had been a second before. It blasted over the stream in sheets of white spray and was gone.

5

Moments later, the hunters paused by the same little stream. They stooped, panting, hands on knees, looking towards the mammoth and the rest of its herd growing ever smaller in the distance.

'What . . . on earth . . .' gasped Daev, 'made you . . . throw your spears . . . at that . . . monster?'

'Big tusks . . . small ears,' wheezed Kehn.

Daev looked up at him in spent disbelief. 'What?'

'Big tusks, small ears,' croaked Aydn. 'Like you said.'

'I said small tusks, big ears! Small tusks, big ears! How could you possibly get that round the wrong way? And didn't we decide to go for a medium-sized mammoth? Medium! What, in any way, was medium about that?'

'They all look big when you're up close,' said Dann.

'And the thicket was really thick,' said Murri.

'That wasn't the only thing,' muttered Leeum.

Dann looked hurt. 'At least we hit it with one spear.'

'Yes,' said Daev with a level stare, 'and has that slowed it down? Where are the other spears?'

'We missed.'

They looked down at the shattered bank and trampled vegetation.

'OK then, let's keep going,' said Daev wearily. 'It has to get tired eventually.'

Dann's eyes went wide. 'Keep going? Are you

kidding? We're lucky to be alive. Surely we've done enough.'

'Then you can be the one that goes back home to tell Mayv we've given up and there won't be any mammoth stuff.'

'Ah,' said Dann.

'I think I'd rather chase mammoths,' said Leeum.

They shared out their remaining spears and walked along the bank to find a place to cross the stream. As they picked their way over some rocks, Aydn looked back at where they had stopped.

'I might be being daft, but did anyone notice someone standing in front of that mammoth, just before it went through the stream? It sort of looked a bit like Nell.'

The hunters paused in their tracks and looked at him.

'You're right,' said Daev. 'Daft.'

Nell splashed and spluttered in the fast-flowing water.

'I can't – *gurgle* – swim.'

It pulled her and spun her and bashed her against submerged rocks.

'Ow! *Gurgle.*'

She tried to grab at the bank but was dragged away. It was freezing. The water was in her eyes; everything was blurry. And she kept going under.

'*Gurgle.*'

Where was Cave Bear?

A brown shape loomed close and she reached for it. Fur! Then another rock knocked them apart.

'Cave Bear!'

Then, again, there he was, closer. She gripped at his fur once more, with both hands this time. She held on tight as together they were washed downstream.

The water calmed a little and Cave Bear
made for the side, swimming as strongly as
he could with Nell holding on round his
shoulders. The current was still fierce but
the bank was getting closer.

Then it was gone.

The bank was gone.

All Cave Bear and Nell could see was
water, just a huge expanse of flat muddy
water.

The little stream had swept them out into
the middle of the big river.

Cave Bear was a strong swimmer, but it
was hard to swim with someone clinging
on to him. The river flowed more slowly
than the stream but it was much, much
wider. He'd been paddling for ages and still

seemed to be no nearer the riverside. He was getting tired.

Nell could feel him slowing down. 'You OK, little guy?'

Cave Bear glanced back at his friend reassuringly. Then he noticed a long low black shape in the water behind her. He stared and coughed a sort of bark.

Nell turned too. And there, just a few splashes away, was a floating log.

From low in the water the drifting shape looked enormous, its stumpy roots sticking out at one end and a few broken branches along its side. They drifted alongside and pulled themselves up on to the ancient tree. They could easily have stood up on the wide trunk, even though most of it was under water.

But for now they sat, dripping, exhausted and happy to be safe.

6

'This is perfect, Cave Bear,' said Nell, looking around. 'We are going at exactly the same speed as the water but we're not having to run to keep up.'

Cave Bear shook the last few drops from his fur and looked at Nell in total agreement.

They were beginning to warm up. Nell

and Cave Bear might have been in the middle of a massive river but the top of the log was out of the water and quite dry. The sun was bright. And they weren't drowning. All in all, not a bad situation, Nell thought.

They found a comfortable spot, leaning back on the stump of a branch, and watched the riverside glide by – the reeds and willows, ducks and dragonflies, the running men and the mammoths. Wait. Men? Mammoths? Could they be Daev and the others? If so, they were a long way behind the mammoths.

'See, Cave Bear. We were right to run away. That lot are never going to catch one of those things. You would have been given to the Sea Clan for sure.'

They sat back in the certain knowledge
that they were doing the right thing.

'Meow.'

Nell and Cave Bear jumped and stared,
astonished. Beside them was a tiny wildcat
kitten. It was completely unfazed, just
sitting and watching the strange
race between man

and mammoth like it was the most natural thing in the world.

'Hello, little cat,' said Nell, and reached out a gentle hand. The kitten's mottled grey fur looked so soft. The tiny creature narrowed its eyes and hissed a tiny hiss. Cave Bear leant over to give the kitten a sniff. The next hiss was louder. But the kitten didn't move. It seemed perfectly happy drifting with its fellow passengers on the river.

'How did you get here?' Nell wondered aloud. 'You couldn't have swum out to the log. Did you fall in the river like us? Or were you on the log the whole time?'

Nell peered into the hole at the end of the branch stump. It certainly looked cosy enough. 'Maybe this old tree was your home. Well, if you've been on the log since it fell in the river, whenever that was, you must be starving.'

She swung her bag in front of her and pulled out some not-so-dry strips of dried elk meat and some soggy nuts and berries.

'I think we're all a bit hungry, little one,' she said.

Nell broke a strip of meat into pieces and laid them out in front of the kitten. She passed Cave Bear a handful of hazelnuts and fruit and took another strip of elk for herself. Soon all three were feeling a lot less hungry and a lot more comfortable. Nell's deerskin tunic and trousers were nearly dry, her boots too.

The river flowed, the log drifted and the hunters chased.

On the far side of the river a hunter from a different tribe had noticed the mammoths and the men and the log drifting by.

Dark eyes under a greasy brow stared. And a crooked smile under a snotty nose whispered, 'Bear.'

7

Before Eava could finish preparing the
vegetables, she'd been interrupted by
Moyrra to help with the eggs. There
was so much going on in the cave that
settling down to do one thing at a time
was virtually impossible. So after the egg-
collecting, childminding, a bit of fur-folding
and a lengthy conversation with Jain about
the pros and cons of packing both pairs of
her bison-hide boots for the hunting trip,
Eava finally sat back down by the food

bowls and chopping boards. She picked up a handful of leeks and looked around for a water bag.

'Hmmf,' she said. Then: 'Has anyone seen Nell?'

The others nearby looked up blankly, glanced around a few times, then shook their heads. 'Nope.'

'Hmmf,' she said again, but not crossly. Poor Nell had been running around for everyone that morning. She'd probably been given yet another job to do.

Eava picked her way up to the wide opening of the cave where Soo and Mayv were talking about mammoth skins.

'Have either of you seen Nell?'

'Um. Not since earlier,' Soo said. 'She came past with an armful of water bags. I haven't seen her since. Come to think of it, I haven't seen Cave Bear either.'

Mayv crossed her arms. 'Ha. Is that why I haven't had that furry nuisance under my feet recently? They're probably still down by the spring, hiding from work, I'll bet.'

Eava frowned at Mayv. 'I'll go and take a look.'

She set off down the shelf of rock to the path at the bottom and walked the little way round to the pool. No Nell. No Cave Bear. Just four empty bags in a neat pile by the water's edge.

'That's odd.'

Then she heard voices. Mayv and Soo were still talking about what to do with the skins the hunters were bringing back.

'But we'll have no time to prepare them,'

Soo was saying. 'They'll still be a bit, er,
fresh.'

'Nonsense,' said Mayv. 'A mammoth skin
is still a prize – and a much better present
than a pet bear!'

Eava stared up at where the conversation
was coming from then back down at the
pool. There were footprints in the damp
earth beside the water – mostly near the
bags – but two sets of prints went along the
edge of the pool to where it trickled out
into a tiny stream that then disappeared
into the woods. One set of prints made
by boots and one set made by paws. Eava

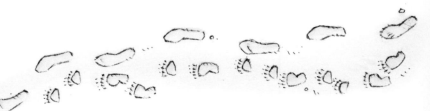

looked up again towards the voices drifting
down from above.

'Oh no,' she whispered, and ran back to
the cave.

It was getting harder to see the hunters now.
The bank was higher and the river itself
was looping away from the chase towards a
great gloomy woodland on the other side.
But the sun was warm, their clothes and fur
had dried, insects zipped, swallows dipped,
fish leapt and splashed. It was fun.

First they were runaways, then
explorers, now intrepid

adventurers out to see the world. Nell had almost forgotten that the point of their journey was to stop Cave Bear from being given away, or that they'd nearly been trampled and drowned. This had become a voyage of discovery – following the stream, wherever it went.

Nell peered at the vast flow they were adrift upon. 'Which bit of water here do you think is ours, Cave Bear? It all looks so brown. None of it looks like the lovely

clear water from the cave pool. I wonder where it's gone. I wonder where the other bits of water have come from. It would take an awful lot of little streams like ours to make a river this big. Cave Bear?'

But Cave Bear was too busy playing with the kitten.

After their little snack and a bit of mammoth-watching the wildcat kitten had curled up in a purring ball on Nell's lap and gone to sleep. Now she was a fizzing bundle of energy, bouncing up and down

the old tree chasing after buzzing bugs and leaping fish. Being an only-bear, Cave Bear had never had another animal to play with. Pets were not the Cave Clan thing.

Nell smiled and watched the two new friends tumble and jump. They were, after all, only a cub and a kitten. Admittedly Cave Bear was much bigger, and Nell could see he was trying not to be too rough with his young playmate. But just then a small trout flapped out of the water and on to the log. The tiny cat froze, then slowly sank flat on to the log, fixing the fish with an unmoving stare as it tried to flip itself back into the water. The kitten swished its tail slightly and made a strange low whirring sound. Then it shot at the fish in a flash of fur and teeth and needle-sharp claws. In a moment there was nothing left of the trout but a piece of fin and a sprinkle of silver scales.

The kitten calmly sat and licked its paws one by one, then sauntered over to where Nell was sitting, climbed up on to her lap, turned round a few times and promptly fell back to sleep again.

Nell and Cave Bear exchanged a nervous look.

8

Gordn, Soo and Porl trudged back up the rock-slab terrace of the cave.

'No sign,' said Soo to the waiting gathering.

'Well, lots of signs,' corrected Porl. 'We found their tracks, but no Nell and no Cave Bear. It looks like they followed the cave stream all the way down through the woods.'

'We called and called but there was no answer,' added Gordn.

'I guess we shouldn't be surprised,' said Eava. 'If they did get all the way to the edge of the woods, it would have been hours ago. They'd be long gone.'

'That's what we thought,' said Soo, 'so we came back.' She looked around at the worried faces. 'That means she's out on the meadows somewhere.'

No one said anything. They knew what that meant. Nell and Cave Bear were exactly where Daev and the others were planning to drive the herd of mammoths.

No one said anything, except Mayv. She waved a dismissive hand. 'Nell will be fine – she's a big girl now. The men have probably already caught their lovely big meaty mammoth higher up the valley.'

Eava stared hard at Mayv. 'How do you know? If they had, we would have heard by now. And anyway, the other mammoths could still be charging down through the meadows.'

'You worry too much. It's only been half a day. Nell's been to the hunting grounds every year of her life – and that trip takes

weeks. If she and that bear are smart
enough to stay out of the way of the hunt,
how much trouble could she really be in?'

Down the valley and across the river, the
Woodland Clan's rough circle
of low bark-covered
shelters crouched

under dark trees in a shallow bowl of
earth and leaves. At the centre a group of
sullen-looking men and women sat round
a meagre fire complaining about having
nothing to eat. Occasionally one of them
poked the fire with a stick, as if their
hunger was all the puny flames'
fault. They wore
shabby bearskin

clothes on their unwashed bodies and tatty bear-claw jewellery round their grubby necks. They smelled terrible.

One of their clan emerged from the surrounding trees and stepped into the smoky ring.

'I've just seen a bear,' he said.

Everybody looked up.

'It was on the river, sitting on a floating log.'

The oldest of the group scowled. 'How big?'

The man blinked. 'The log or the bear?'

'The bear, of course!'

'It's a little one – a cub,' said the man. 'It's with a girl and a cat.'

If the others thought this arrangement of individuals sitting on a floating log in the middle of a river seemed odd, no one mentioned it. They were all far too busy thinking about the bear cub.

The older man smiled. 'A little one, eh? We can fatten him up soon enough.'

Softly, everyone began chanting, 'Bear, bear, bear.'

Then louder: 'Bear! Bear! Bear!'

The older man rose, stooping, to his feet. 'The river will bring him to us. Get the cage, get the ropes,' he snarled. 'To the canoes! We're going on a bear hunt. We're going to catch a little one.'

9

Just like the tiny stream that Nell and Cave Bear followed from the cave, the mighty river had once been an unimportant trickle. High in the white mountains, beyond the great plain, it had begun its long journey as no more than a few drops of melted snow. But, like the tiny stream, it had grown and grown – joined by other trickles, other torrents and, finally, other rivers.

Out on the plain it fed the vast grey lake that the Lakeside people lived beside. It then swept onwards, past the big forest and into the canyon at the top of the Cave Clan's valley. Down on the broad valley floor, the river twisted this way and that in great loops and curves.

Having bent towards the woodland, the river swung round once more and returned over the meadows, right across the path of the fleeing mammoths, cutting off their escape.

Daev slowed his run and pointed with his spear. 'They've stopped! They're caught in the curve of the river – and left or right brings them back towards us. They're trapped.'

The men halted, breathing hard, and looked ahead.

'I think I liked it better when they were running away from us,' panted Dann.

Daev put a hand on his shoulder. 'Come on, you want to be a hunter, don't you? Get a mammoth and you'll be a hero. This is our chance.'

'I guess,' said Dann.

'And Mayv will be happy,' added Leeum.

The other hunters nodded approvingly.

'Right, let's spread out in a line and slowly push the mammoths further towards the bend in the river. They'll be hemmed in on all sides with nowhere to go. We can pick out that medium one we wanted and close in. Got that?'

More nodding.

'Leeum and Caal, you go that side. I'll take this side with Dann and Aydn. Kehn, Roj and Murri in between. And please, everyone, SMALL TUSKS, BIG EARS.'

For the first time since pulling themselves out of the river, Nell did not like the view from the log. On one side high banks meant she couldn't see the open meadows any more, while, on the other, a murky curtain of trees appeared to close in over them.

Spooky branches reached out over the water and thick undergrowth hid whatever

lurked within. Everything seemed to give off a cold frightening whisper. Cave Bear and the kitten looked uneasy too. The kitten hissed at a scary-looking bush and even Cave Bear did a little growl when he thought he saw something move behind a tree. But at last the darkness was breaking up and the woodland gave way to grassland again.

The three companions watched the last twisted tree glide by. Nell shivered then smiled. 'I'm glad that's behind us.'

Cave Bear returned the smile – or did what passed as smiling for bears. But, as Nell glanced back at the receding gloom, in the distance she saw a long shape slide out of the shadows of overhanging trees into

the middle of the river. Then another. And another.

Three low, long, thin boats were now in the water behind them, each holding three or four people. They dipped flat-ended sticks into the river and the boats turned. All three pointed directly at the log.

Nell, Cave Bear and the kitten stared upstream at the little boats following them. They could see the people, but not closely enough to know who they were.

'What do you think, Cave Bear? Are they coming to rescue us? Do you think they're coming to take us back to the cave?'

A note of worry crept into Nell's voice. The reason for running away in the first place was suddenly very clear. But the more they watched, the more it seemed that these people were not coming to help. They didn't wave and they didn't call out. They just paddled silently towards the log.

'I don't like the look of

this,' Nell said. 'Those boat things came out of that horrible woodland. I've heard Mayv and the others talk about the Woodland Clan. Do you think this is them?'

Cave Bear appeared not to hear. Instead, he and the kitten were listening to something else, their ears pricked.

'What is it, boy?'

They were gathered at the end of the log closest to the canoes, standing by the stumpy roots of the old tree. Nell leant forward, squinting back up the river. Now she thought she caught something. A murmur. Each time the paddle sticks hit the water there was a breath of a sound.

'Air, air, air.'

The canoes began to close the gap. Nell

could see faces. Unfriendly, hungry-looking faces. And the sound was louder now too, more like 'pair, pair, pair'.

Then, with horror, Nell realised it wasn't 'pair, pair, pair' – it was 'bear, bear, bear'!

The kitten hissed and the three friends began to inch away from the end of the log. Nell saw that the paddles were driving the canoes forward much faster than the river was carrying the log. She knelt down and paddled as fast as she could with her hands but it had absolutely no effect – the ancient log was just too wide, too long and too heavy.

She looked over her shoulder and saw how close one of the canoes had come. She let out a frightened yelp, snatched up

the kitten and
ran to the front
end of the log,
Cave Bear close
behind. There was
nowhere else to go.

She and Cave Bear might survive a swim
to the side but she didn't think the kitten
would. Anyway, the closest bank was now
as high and steep as a cliff, and on the
other side the first canoe was nearly level
with the log.

Nell stared with rising panic at the
smirking, chanting faces.

'What do you want?'

'Bear, bear, bear!' was the only reply.

She pulled Cave Bear tight and held on

to one of the old tree's short branches where the kitten now perched, completely still, its eyes narrowed.

'Bear, bear, bear!'

The canoe pulled alongside, the first man only a few feet away. He put down his paddle and reached out towards Cave Bear.

Nell unslung her food bag and started whacking the man with it.

'You can't' – *whack!* – 'have him.' Whack! But with the next whack the man grabbed the bag, ripped it from Nell's grasp and flung it in the river.

'Ha!' He lunged across and caught Cave Bear by the back leg. 'Got you, my yummy little snack.'

Nell screamed and tried to pull her friend

the other way. Cave Bear twisted round and bit.

'Ow! That hurt. I'll show you!'

The man reached for his paddle and raised it, ready to strike. Then, out of the corner of his eye, he noticed a swish of tail and heard a strange low whirring sound.

In a flash of fury and needle-sharp claws the kitten launched herself at the man's face.

'Ow, ow! Get it off!' As teeth cut and claws tore, he let go of Cave Bear and tried to lift the flailing banshee from his head. 'Ow!'

The second man in the canoe laughed. 'Don't be such a wimp; it's only a ki— Ow!' he wailed, as the tiny ball of rage sprang next on to him. 'Ow!'

'Hold still, I'll get it,' said the woman sitting behind him, and she swung her paddle at the kitten. But the kitten leapt mid-swing and landed, claws first, on top of her head. 'Oww!'

An instant later, the swinging paddle connected loudly with the second man's ear. *CRACK!*

'Oooowww!' The kitten then shot on to

the head of the last paddler, who happened
to be bald.

'Ooww!'

With a parting bite the little cat leapt
from the now retreating boat and landed
elegantly back on the log.

10

As the first canoe drifted away the other
two Woodland Clan canoes moved closer.
One contained the man who had seen
Cave Bear in the first place and the grizzled
older man who led the hunt.

Seeing what had happened to the
leading boat, he changed plans. 'Get your
ropes,' he barked. 'Go either side. Lasso the
log. We'll have them then. But keep your
distance.'

The kitten bounced back to the front of

the log where Cave Bear and Nell were waiting.

'You really are a wild little wildcat, aren't you?'

Nell picked up the ferocious fluffball and hugged her to her chest. 'Thank you for saving Cave Bear.'

The kitten purred a 'you're welcome' kind of purr.

But just then Nell felt a nudge on her leg. Cave Bear was pointing with his snout. The other canoes were closing in. There was a cage in one of them. On each boat a man swung a looped rope over his head. As the canoes came closer the men pitched their ropes at the log, aiming for the stumpy roots at the far end. One missed, splashing into the river. The other fell round a root and pulled tight. Nell felt a slight jolt beneath her feet. Another rope came over, looping a branch, then another.

'Bear, bear, bear!' came the chant again.

The boats on either side were close enough now for Nell to see twisted grins and yellow teeth. The older Woodland Clan man half stood and opened the top of the cage behind him.

'We only want the bear,' he sneered. 'You can keep the cat.'

The others sniggered.

Another rope attached itself to a branch

right where Nell was standing. She tried to dislodge it, but it was yanked tight.

The old man banged the side of the cage. 'Give me the bear!'

'Never!' she cried. 'Never!'

'Fine. Then we'll take him.'

She looked around desperately but it was hopeless.

The canoes drew nearer.

'Bear, bear, bear!'

Then, with a slight whistle, a spear came

hurtling down from the bright blue sky above and plunged straight through the centre of the nearest canoe. Water gushed from the hole.

The Woodland Clan crew yelped. 'Eek!'

Another spear sailed over their heads into the river.

'Eeeek!'

The canoe started to settle lower in the water.

'What's happening?' growled the older man, as yet another spear narrowly missed the sinking boat.

'We're under attack!' yelled the man who'd first seen Cave Bear.

Suddenly the heavens were split by a thunderous, trumpeting bellow.

Everyone looked up, dumbstruck, to see a colossal mammoth high on the riverbank, holding a spear in its trunk. 'We're under attack — by mammoths!'

cried the man.

With a casual swing the mammoth threw the spear into the river.

Everyone watched as it arched gracefully through the air towards the older man's canoe. He shrieked and fell back heavily into the cage as the spear disappeared with a silent splash beside him. Only his legs poked out from the top.

That was quite enough for the Woodland Clan.

'That's it, I'm off,' said one.

'First cats, now mammoths,' said another.

'Let's get out of here,' said everybody else.

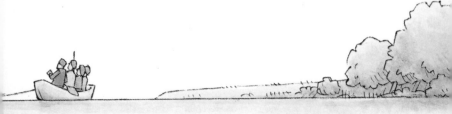

They let go of the ropes, thrust their paddles into the water and turned their canoes back the way they had come.

A pair of angry eyes glared out from inside the cage but there was nothing the hunt leader could do. There was one more mighty trumpet from above and the canoes all leapt forward, paddles paddling even faster.

Soon they were just long low shapes in the distance, one of them distinctly lower than the others.

Nell looked up at the high bank, but the river had already carried the log onwards and there was no sign of the mammoth that had rescued them.

11

Moments before, up on the meadows, the line of Cave Clan hunters trying to push the mammoths back towards the river had closed in. The mammoths were milling about in alarm, making it difficult for the men to single out the medium-sized one with the big ears and the small tusks.

The biggest animals stood between the hunters and the rest of the herd. One of them was the massive beast they'd seen at the little stream, still with a spear sticking out from a shoulder. It swung its terrifying tusks from side to side in great grass-swishing sweeps.

'Are we sure about this?' squeaked Dann.

Daev didn't even glance across. 'Shhh.'

The men edged forward, spears poised for throwing. At last the medium mammoth they wanted moved off to the side, nearer Daev's end of the line. This was their chance.

'Now!' he called in a harsh whisper.

He stood up and launched his spear. But, just as he threw, the mammoth turned back to the rest of the herd. The spear sailed

harmlessly past the retreating animal's
rump and disappeared into the river below.
As did Aydn's – and then Dann's.

Daev stared across at them, hands out
wide. 'What did you do that for? He's
gone!'

'I panicked,' said Dann. 'Anyway, you
missed too.'

'But at least it was there when I threw,'
answered Daev, pointing.

But as he pointed he
saw that where
the medium

mammoth had been the giant mammoth was now standing, staring down at them from nearly twice a hunter's height. It slowly turned its head, reached back with its trunk and plucked the spear from its side. It lifted it high in the air and let out an ear-shattering roar, then slung the spear away.

Somewhere, someone shrieked.

'We're going to die,' piped Dann.

The mighty mammoth with the little ears and absolutely enormous tusks grumbled a deep growl and the rest of the herd slowly turned and faced the hunters.

'Oops,' said Daev.

With one more deafening bellow the mammoths lowered their massive heads – and charged.

12

All was quiet on the river, apart from the fading rumble of stampeding mammoths. Not that Nell could hear. Her heart was thumping too much.

'What's going on, Cave Bear? First a mammoth tries to squish us, then we get washed away, then we're saved by a log with a kitten on it, then we're attacked by angry people in canoes, and then we get rescued by the same mammoth that tried to kill us. What next?'

She slumped down on the log. 'All

I wanted to do was stop Mayv giving you away. Instead, what happens? I nearly get you trampled, drowned and captured. I'm sorry, Cave Bear.'

She put an arm round her friend. 'Maybe we should just go home. We could find

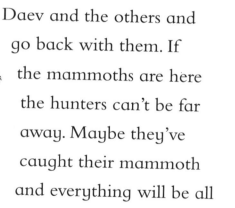

Daev and the others and go back with them. If the mammoths are here the hunters can't be far away. Maybe they've caught their mammoth and everything will be all

right.' She glanced up at the high bank. 'Or maybe they haven't. Where did those spears come from? If they were ours, it looks like they missed. And if they haven't caught a mammoth, we'll be back where we started from and they'll give you to the Sea Clan. Oh, Cave Bear – I don't know what to do. And the food's gone.'

Cave Bear rested his head on Nell's shoulder and the kitten climbed up on to her lap.

'And you, little kitten, what about you? If Mayv doesn't like pet cave bears, I don't suppose she's going to like pet wildcats.'

Nell looked down at the big eyes looking back at her and felt Cave Bear's soft muzzle at her neck. She made a decision.

'Right,' she said, straightening up. 'There's nothing for it – we have to keep going. We started following the water, wherever it went, and that's what we're going to do. Wherever it goes. Adventurers to the end.'

Cave Bear looked back at her as if to say 'And friends forever'.

The kitten calmly licked her paws in absolute agreement.

They floated on in silence, the ropes drifting alongside like curling ribbons and a spear or two bobbing nearby. The river twisted and turned, wider now and slower, the banks lower, with tall rushes creeping out into the current from the water's edge. Now and then they caught glimpses of the meadows again, and once Nell fancied she saw the hunters and the mammoths still running down the valley.

That's strange, she thought. Daev and the men are in front.

But she didn't wonder for long. The

warm afternoon sun and slow lapping water soon soothed any troubled thoughts and before long the three explorers were feeling more than a little bit drowsy.

Nell leant back against a branch, the kitten on her lap and Cave Bear by her side – and fell asleep.

Soo and Eava stood on the terrace,
looking out across the treetops at the
grassland and the river beyond. Behind
them they could hear Mayv ordering
people about, preparing for the arrival of a
mammoth's worth of meat, tusks and furs.

'No, no. Put the drying racks right at the
back of the cave where it's cooler. We'll start
preparing the skins and drying the meat
tomorrow. No, not there! Further back.'

The two women exchanged a glance
and stared back over the woods.

'If Nell was hurt, Daev would have found
her and brought her home,' Soo said.

'Definitely,' Eava added, trying to sound optimistic. 'One of them would surely bring her back. Or perhaps she's helping with the hunt – you know, carrying spears for them or something.'

Soo nodded quickly. 'Yes, that'll be it. She and Cave Bear are probably dragging some great hunk of mammoth back here with the others as we speak. Maybe Mayv is right. They'll be home soon.'

They gave each other a smile but turned and looked at the wide valley again.

'I want to go and look for them,' said Eava.

'Me too,' said Soo.

In the winter the low late-day sun reached deep into the furthest parts of the cave. Now, in mid-spring, it only shone as far as the cooking fires. But the busy workers were still lit by a golden afternoon glow that bounced around the rocky walls.

Mayv was talking and pointing as Soo and Eava approached.

'We want to go and look for Nell and Cave Bear,' said Soo.

Mayv turned. 'What?'

'We'll pick up their trail easily enough.'

Mayv shook her head. 'No, no, we're far too busy here. We've got to get ready for when the men return with all the mammoth goodies. Nell will be fine.'

'You don't know that,' said Soo.

'And you don't know if the hunters will come back with anything,' added Eava.

'You're just hoping they do.'

Everyone else stopped lifting things and listened.

Soo pointed to the mouth of the cave. 'What if she's injured out there somewhere? She's been gone for hours.'

'And so have the hunters,' said Eava. 'If they'd caught a mammoth before the little stream like they planned, they'd be bringing it home by now.'

'Sounds about right,' muttered Gordn.

Mayv flashed him a silencing look.
'Butchering a mammoth is not easy – it
takes a lot of time. We might not see them
for a while yet.'

More muttering and mumbling spread
through the group.

Mayv glanced around. 'All right, all
right. Go if you must. I'm sure you're
wasting your time. But if you are going,
I suggest you go quickly. The sun's already
getting low.'

'Thank you, Mayv,' said Eava and Soo
together as they hurried back up the cave.
They threw some food in a bag, snatched
up a fur blanket and dashed out across the
terrace and down into the woods.

13

Nell woke up with a jolt. For a moment she was unsure where she was. Then it all came back . . . water, river, log, kitten.

She smiled and stretched her arms.
'I wonder where we are now?'

She wobbled to her feet and took a few steps to the end of the log where Cave Bear and the kitten were sitting, seemingly lost in silent conversation as they gazed out at the scene before them. The landscape downriver was different – wider, flatter and much more orange.

'The sun's going down, Cave Bear. And we still haven't got to wherever it is the water goes.'

She looked around at the darkening reeds and redder sky, hands on hips. 'I hope this river knows where it's going.'

But the river simply continued its slow turning tour of directions. A heron flapped lazily into the air. Frogs began to click and croak. An arrowhead of birds flew over, honking high above. There was a faint burble.

'Sorry, that was my tummy,' said Nell.

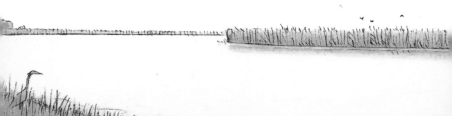

'I guess we've had nothing to eat for ages.'
She knelt down and picked up the kitten.
'Except for you, of course. You had that fish.
And a bit of bear hunter, maybe.'

A contented meow was all the reply she
got.

Apart from being hungry, or eager to get
where they were going, something else was
nagging at Nell. Something she couldn't
quite put her finger on. She'd never been
on the river before. Besides, with the setting
sun, everything looked strange. And yet

something felt familiar. Was it the air? Did the reedy, muddy-river smell seem somehow fresher? Nell couldn't tell. Perhaps it was a sound. Just beyond the calls of the frogs and nesting birds, was there a sort of a hushed low boom now and then?

Nell peered ahead, listening carefully.

Even though the sun had dipped below the far hills on the other side of the river, Soo and Eava could clearly see the little trail of trampled grass running alongside the stream.

'This had to be Nell and Cave Bear,' said Eava, studying the tracks by the bank. 'See? Paw prints. But they don't go on any further.'

Soo was looking at another set of tracks. 'But this was a mammoth. And over the other side too. Look at them. It must have been enormous.' She stared at the flattened bank.

Then Eava pointed. 'Look! More prints: men, the hunters. You can see where they stopped. The little holes made by the ends of their spears. And after the mammoth had been through here, by the look of it.'

'Then Nell's OK,' sighed Soo. 'If she'd been hurt, and Daev and the men were here, we'd know by now. She must have gone on with them. And see? Their tracks continue on the other side.'

'So all we have to do is catch up with the hunt. If a mammoth was here and the hunters were close behind, they can't be far away. Let's go.'

Soo and Eava picked their way over the very same rocks the hunters had crossed a few hours before and ran on into the gathering dusk.

Nell was holding the kitten, and she had an arm round Cave Bear too. It was darker now, and cooler, but that wasn't the reason the three of them were in a huddle.

The riverside was all shadow and the river itself had turned the same purple-blue as the sky, but that wasn't what was scary. Nor were the night-time cries of unseen animals and birds.

It was the other sound. It was clear now, the dull boom – sometimes two or three in a row. And with each bend of the river the sound was louder.

'I know we're brave adventurers and everything,' she whispered, 'ever so brave, but where is the water going? Why is it taking us towards that noise? Every time we've heard things in the distance today they've turned out to be not very nice.'

She'd forgotten about being hungry. She was trying hard not to be scared. But as the last of the twilight sank into night and the booms became crashes, not being scared was getting much, much harder.

'We're brave adventurers, Cave Bear, very brave, ever so very br— Oh.'

The mighty river turned one last time. In the dim light Nell saw the dark riverbanks turn into pale and distant dunes while in front, as wide as the wide night sky, was a vast, crashing, booming blackness.

They had reached the sea.

14

'What is that?' squeaked Nell, struggling to
find the words. 'Is that all water? It can't be.
It's so big. It's . . . it's everywhere.'

Huge waves were rising towards the river
mouth, their towering crests turning white
before toppling over into crashing storms
of foam.

'So that's what the noise is. All that
tumbling water. And that's where this water
is going – to join up with all that water.
And the log. And us!' Still holding the kitten,

Nell took Cave Bear's paw and retreated back along the log. The branch they once sat against in the lazy sunshine, they now clung to in growing unease.

Soon they were swept out beyond the beach. The log bumped and rocked in a chaos of rough water where the river met the waves.

'Hold tight, Cave Bear!' shouted Nell over the roar of the surf. 'It's like being in the little stream again. We're getting wet – again. Urgh! It's salty. Why is it salty?'

But Cave Bear was far too busy hanging on to answer.

Suddenly a peak of white froth broke over them. Nell's hand slipped from

the branch and was left clutching at air as
she lost her balance.

She began to fall. But then her fingertips
brushed something and gripped. It was
a rope. One of the ropes thrown by
the Woodland Clan, still tied
to the branch. Nell
hauled herself

back upright again beside Cave Bear with the petrified kitten still in her arms, and gasped at the cold shock of the water.

'I nearly lost you!' she cried. 'What are we going to do? I don't think I can hold you and hold on at the same time.' She stared helplessly at her friends as another foaming wave pulled at their legs.

The kitten meowed a 'that's all right' sort of meow and simply climbed out of Nell's hug on to the branch and disappeared down the hole at the end.

'Of course,' said Nell. 'Your old home. It's the perfect place.'

A happy but more muffled meow came from inside.

With the kitten safely in her den, Nell and Cave Bear wrapped their arms round the branch and each other, as the log pitched and rolled through the wild water that took the river out to sea.

'This water is too bouncy,' spat Nell. 'And too salty.'

However, the choppy splashing soon gave way to the steady rise and fall of much larger waves.

'And it's too big!'

All they could see now against the dark sky and inky-black water were each other's frightened eyes – and occasionally the pale sand of the beach whenever a wave lifted them high enough. The log seemed to have drifted, parallel with the shoreline, away from the mouth of the river.

'Where are we going now, Cave Bear? It's dark and we're wet and frozen – and I think I might like to stop following the water soon.' Nell peered into the hole at the end of the branch. 'And what about you, little cat? You've been on the log longest of all.'

Another muffled meow came in reply.

Then, with the next rolling rise,

Nell noticed that the beach appeared to be closer. The waves were definitely steeper and the sound of the surf louder.

'Cave Bear, look! Do you think the water heard me?'

Another huge wave took them higher than ever. It seemed like they could see the coastline stretch out for miles. They paused for a tiny moment at the top, suspended in the night. Then the crest of the wave tipped forward.

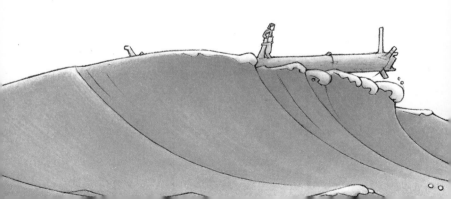

'Cave Bear?'

And they fell – wave, ancient tree, passengers and all.

'Caaaave Beaarrrr!'

Nell and Cave Bear were swept off the log in a churning confusion of water and

noise. In the tumbling surf it was impossible to know which way was up. Nell was spun in somersaults. Her lungs burst for air. But, with one last fit of thrashing legs and splashing arms, she found the surface, gasping.

'I – still – can't – swim! *Gurgle.*'

The foaming white of the wave carried Nell and Cave Bear towards the beach.

'I – really – still – can't – sw— Oh, I don't need to.'

Her feet had touched the bottom. For the first time for hours Nell felt something under her that wasn't a tree.

Another surge of water threw her out on to wet sand, coughing, spluttering and eyes stinging. Nell and Cave Bear lay there for

a second, catching their breath and feeling
the beach beneath them. Behind them the
old log, huge and black, lay stranded in the
wash. On either side the shoreline curved
away into the distance.

In front was a pair of bare feet.

'Hello,' said a kindly voice. 'Are you
all right?'

15

Nell looked up and
saw a tall young woman
looking down at her.
    'Are you all right?' asked
the woman again.

Nell slowly got to her feet. 'I think so.'

'You poor thing. What's your name? How did you get here?'

'I'm Nell and this is Cave Bear,' said Nell, somewhat dazed. 'We were on a log but we got washed off.'

She turned and pointed at the dark shape behind her. But the young woman didn't seem interested in the log.

'Nell?' she asked. 'Little Nell? Cousin Nell? From the cave? What on earth are you doing on our beach?'

Nell's already bewildered head spun. 'What? Cousin? Your beach? Who are you? Where am I?'

'I'm Alsa,' said the woman, 'from the Sea Clan. This is where I live.'

Nell stared up, horrified, as what Alsa had said sank in.

The Sea Clan!

After everything they'd been through, running away from the cave, following the stream, in the stream, on the log, fighting off the Woodland Clan, being swept out to sea – everything to keep Cave Bear from being given away – Nell had brought her friend to the very people she was trying so hard to keep him away from.

It was too much. She sank to the sand beside Cave Bear. 'Noooo!' she cried. 'No. We're together. You can't have him! You can't have him!'

Alsa knelt down in front of them. 'Nell, Nell, it's OK. Don't be upset. What are you talking about?'

Nell pulled her friend close. 'Cave Bear. Mayv said she was going to give Cave Bear to the Sea Clan as a present when they visited the cave. It's tradition. Furs or tools or ivory or pets. So we ran away and the river carried us down the valley and now we're here. And you're going to take Cave Bear to be a pet, but he's my friend.'

A tear glinted in the dark.

Alsa reached out and hugged them both. 'Oh, Nell, no. We'll never take your friend from you. Do you understand? We wouldn't do that.'

'But Mayv wants to give you a pet. She says you like pets.'

Alsa sat back. 'Pets, yes, we like pets. Little pets. Cave Bear might be small now but he's not going to stay that way, is he? One day he'll be enormous. No, little pets for us – no bears. Something we can fit on our boats – birds, dogs, cats, that sort of thing.'

'Cats!' Nell gasped. 'Oh my gosh!'

She dashed back to the log and climbed up. Then, from a hole at the end of one of the branches, Nell brought out, bedraggled and blinking, the cutest little kitten Alsa had ever seen.

Nell jumped down and walked back. 'Would you like to look after this wildcat kitten for me instead?'

Alsa gazed at the frightened bundle of fur and held it up to her cheek. 'Oh yes,' she said softly. 'I'll take very good care of her. Thank you, Nell.'

The four of them paused, just as they were.

Nell and Cave Bear, Alsa and the kitten.

Waves crashed. The kitten purred. Nell shivered.

Alsa snapped out of the happy moment. 'Goodness, Nell, I'm so sorry – you must be frozen. Quick, let's get you all by a fire and dried out.' She stood up and nodded down the beach. 'Follow me.'

As they walked Nell began to notice points of light in the distance, set against darker night-time shapes.

'They're our huts,' Alsa said. 'But you probably don't remember. You were tiny when you were here last time.'

Nell looked at Alsa, shocked. 'I was here?'

'Absolutely. You came with the rest

of the Cave Clan the last time we all got together.'

'I don't remember.' Nell looked ahead towards the huts. 'But on the river, as it got dark, something . . . something felt familiar.'

'We had a great time,' Alsa continued. 'It was lovely to see everyone again. Mayv and Gordn and Moyrra and everyone.' She held out the kitten. 'And we gave you all sorts of presents – mostly some particularly lovely fish. Look, see? That's what we go fishing in.'

They had reached a row of long wooden boats that had been dragged up the beach away from the waves. They were a bit like the Woodland Clan's canoes but bigger, with higher ends and sides.

However, Nell thought they didn't look nearly big enough. 'You go out there,' she said, pointing at the pounding surf, 'in those?'

Alsa smiled. 'It's all right when you get used to it. The sea can be pretty wild sometimes but it's usually a lot calmer. We go out and hunt for fish the way you hunt for –'

'The hunters!' burst out Nell. 'I'd completely forgotten about the hunters. They were after mammoths. We saw them in the valley. One of the mammoths tried to flatten us. But then it rescued us from the bear hunters in canoes.'

Alsa stared at Nell. 'Canoes? Bear hunters? Rescued by mammoths? What are you talking about?'

Nell waved her hands excitedly. 'I'll tell you later. It doesn't matter now. Mayv was going to give you Cave Bear, but if the hunters got a mammoth, there'd be lots and lots of lovely meat and fur and ivory to give to you as presents.'

'Ah,' said Alsa. 'Let's keep walking. We're nearly home. I know all about your hunters.'

16

Alsa, Nell and Cave Bear walked higher up the beach to where a line of boxy thatched huts sat amongst trees and fishing nets. Most were empty as they went past. All the noise appeared to be coming from a much bigger building set at the centre of the others.

Alsa stopped at a door flanked by tall poles carved with scenes of boats and fish.

'In here,' she said, pulling aside a heavy curtain door.

Cave Bear beside her, Nell stepped

through and joined the crowded hubbub inside. The room was lit by a large fire, but at first all Nell could see were the dark backs of people standing in front of it.

'Excuse me,' said Alsa loudly. 'I found someone else.'

The chatter subsided and the people in front of Nell turned and stepped back, revealing the glowing fire and the eight battered, bruised and bandaged men who sat round it.

'Daev?' said Nell.

'Nell?' said Daev.

'What are you doing here?' they said at the same time.

Nell looked around at the surprised faces of the Cave Clan hunters.

'How –' began Daev, but he was cut short by Alsa.

'That can wait. Right now we have to get these two warm and fed. Budge up, gentlemen, make some room.'

The hunters shuffled along the low benches they were sitting on, and Nell sat down, Cave Bear at her feet.

A grey-haired Sea Clan woman brought fur blankets. She called over her shoulder, 'Erruk, bring another bowl, and something for this little fellow.

He looks famished, poor thing. And I don't suppose bears are meant to be swimming in the sea if that's where you've been, especially at night.'

Alsa joined the circle beside Nell, showing everyone the little wildcat for the first time. 'Or kittens. Can we have something for this one as well?'

The bowls came – vegetables for Cave Bear, fish for the kitten and soup for Nell.

'It's fish too,' she said.

'It's actually really nice,' said Leeum.

Nell looked up at the hunters seated around her. They had furs over their shoulders like her. Empty wooden bowls sat on the sandy floor. Murri's arm was in a sling, Kehn had a leather bandage round his left knee, Caal had one round his head and Dann had the beginnings of a black eye. Roj had lost a boot.

'What happened?' asked Nell through a slurping mouthful.

'The mammoths tried to kill us,' said Dann. 'We chased them all the way down the valley. Then they chased us all the way here. First we caught up with them, then they caught up with us.'

The others nodded.

'It wasn't the big one that did all the damage,' said Daev.

'No,' said Leeum. 'Annoyingly, it was the medium one with the small tusks and big ears.'

'We managed to get

away,' Daev continued, 'and blundered into the trees behind the Sea Clan's village just as the sun went down. Erruk here found us.'

'I was collecting firewood,' said Erruk by way of explanation.

'But, Nell,' said Daev, 'that's how we got here. How on earth did you get here?'

Nell looked down at Cave Bear, who looked back with an expression that Nell took to mean 'Go on then'.

So she told her tale – from overhearing Leeum tell Mayv about the mammoths to being washed up on

the Sea Clan's beach and meeting Alsa.

The whole room went deathly quiet when she got to the bit about the charging giant mammoth. And there were lots of outraged mutterings when she told them about the Woodland Clan's attempt to capture Cave Bear. By the time Nell got to the part about reaching the sea they were simply amazed. Although at one point Aydn was heard to mutter, 'Hmmf, not so daft then.'

Nell suddenly realised how tired she was. 'Could I possibly have another bowl of that yummy soup?'

Lora, the older Sea Clan woman, said, 'Little Nell, after that adventure, you can have whatever you like.'

Nell looked down at her friend. 'It was an adventure, wasn't it, Cave Bear?'

Cave Bear almost certainly agreed.

Nell lifted a spoonful of the fresh soup and watched a drip fall back into the bowl. It was more of a trickle really. 'Oh, and we discovered where the water goes.'

Just then, excited voices were heard coming from outside, and Soo and Eava burst through the curtain door.

'Soo?'

'Daev?'

'Eava?'

'Nell? Oh, Nell, thank goodness you're safe!' gasped Soo. 'Daev, you too, and everyone!' She noticed the bandages. 'Is everybody all right?'

There was some general nodding and mumbling.

Eava looked around. 'Did you find a mammoth?'

'No,' laughed Nell, hugging Cave Bear. 'I found a kitten instead.'

CAVE BEAR CARE

If you want to look after a cave bear, there are a few things you should know.

 Cave bears get big. They are a bit taller than their forest-living brown bear cousins but can be a lot heavier, weighing as much as ten grown-up humans. Perhaps even as much as sixteen!

1 month   3 months   6 months   1 year   fully grown

They are similar in shape and colour to a brown bear but have a more sloping back and a more pronounced forehead.

Cave bears are vegetarian. They might eat the occasional bug or fish but their teeth are designed for chewing plants.

 They hibernate through the winter. Or, more accurately, they go into near-hibernation – like a very, very deep sleep. Make sure you have  somewhere for them to snooze undisturbed. (They might be grumpy if you wake them up.) Also, they don't need the loo while they are hibernating so, for a while at least, there's no clearing up after them.

 To get ready for the big winter sleep they have to eat – a LOT. An adult cave bear can double its weight from spring to the end of autumn. Don't run out of food.

Cave bears are very intelligent and will need interesting things to do and play with.

Although they will happily keep you company during the day, they are most active at dawn and dusk. So there'll be no more sleeping in.

Being intelligent, and having a particularly good sense of smell, a cave bear will be able to find not only it's own food, but your family's food as well. Keep it somewhere a bear can't reach.